THE AMAZING BEES

THE AMAZING BEES

A Children's Theatrical Experience

Concept and Vision by Yoel Silber

gatekeeper press™
Columbus, Ohio

The Amazing Bees: A Children's Theatrical Experience

Illustrated by QBN studios, LLC.

Published by Gatekeeper Press
2167 Stringtown Rd, Suite 109
Columbus, OH 43123-2989
www.GatekeeperPress.com

ISBN (hardcover): 9781662903434
ISBN (paperback): 9781662903441
eISBN: 9781662903458

Library of Congress Control Number: 2020943181

The world we live in is an incredibly precious place. Made up of flowing streams, towering mountains, billowing trees, beautiful flowers, and so much more, millions of species of plants and animals live together on this Earth.

All living things work together to make this ecosystem a place where everybody can live in peace.

Humans, however, sometimes forget about this responsibility and unknowingly cause harm to tiny little beings that can't speak up for themselves.

Honey bees are one of these creatures, and not too long ago, a group of them had the adventure of their lives while working to save their hive from a dangerous force bigger than they'd ever seen before.

This is their story. It is the amazing tale of a few extraordinary bees who teamed up to save their colony. And, as with any story, there has to be a hero, and the hero of this story is a little girl named Princess Debbee.

As you might guess from her name, she's the princess of the honey bee hive, and she lives with her parents King Buzz and Queen Bee, her little brother Prince Bob Bee, and all of the wonderful workers who help produce honey for the entire colony.

Now, it's important to get to know the parts of a princess bee, as they're different from any other princess you've ever known.

A princess bee is just like any regular human girl, but with a dash of honey, sting, and fight in her. The honey makes her sweet, her stinger helps her protect herself, and the fight-well, that's just something all girls seem to be born with, even bee girls.

Like any little princess, Debbee loves to dance. She rocks out in her room to her favorite bee band all the time. As the princess of the beehive, she'll be Queen one day.

Being Queen Bee is hard work, which is why Debbee's mom is making her take lessons to learn everything she needs to know about life as a bee! It sounds fun, but sometimes she gets so worried she won't be able to learn it all in time. That's why she dances!

Knock, knock, knock!

"Ugh, that must be my little brother, Bob Bee,"
the princess exclaims while straightening her
dress and opening the door.

"I saw you dancing!"
shouts Prince Bob Bee.

"I wasn't dancing!"

"Were too!"

"Was not!"

Princess Debbee shakes her little stinger in
the direction of her brother and sticks her
tongue out playfully. Prince Bob Bee looks back
at his own bee-hind. There's no stinger there.

"Still hasn't come in?" asks Princess Debbee.
Boy bees actually don't ever grow stingers. It's

because they don't really need them for the work they do to support the hive. Princess Debbee and Prince Bob Bee, however, will learn this a little bit later.

"I don't want to talk about it," replies Bob Bee. He looks deeply saddened for just a second. "Anyway, Mom is looking for you. It's time for your lesson."

Princess Debbee makes sure that her stinger is straight and her dress is smooth and walks out the door before giving her little brother a small push into the honeycomb walls that line the hallways of the hive.

Princess Debbee and her brother enter the wonderful, golden workroom filled with dripping honey that falls from the boxes that tower all along the walls. A little bit of honey falls onto Bob Bee's nose and he delightfully licks it right up. This is one of the perks of being a honey bee.

A female worker bee rushes past the two little bees.

"I'm going to be late! Off to work," she says hurriedly as she kisses her husband on the cheek.

Her husband puts his drone hat on and waves her goodbye, shouting, "Okay, honey! See you later!"

Girl bees become worker bees in a typical honey bee colony, and it's their job to help gather nectar, guard the honey, care for the Queen, and much, much more. Boy bees become drones, and their jobs are a little different. No matter what a bee's job is, however, there's a place for every single one in the hive.

The worker bee joins her group of female co-workers as the male drones fall into line. Queen Bee, the beautiful ruler of the hive, rises from her throne to greet her two children. Her honey bee dress flows regally behind her and drapes over her eggs as she gracefully walks down the stairs.

"You're a little late to today's lesson," the Queen whispers to Princess Debbee.

Bob Bee butts in, "It was because she was dancing to that silly boy bee band again. What's it called, Debbee? The Buzzy Bee Bump?"

Princess Debbee thumps her little brother in the bee-hind and continues walking with her mother.

As the three walk through the honeycomb workroom, the sunlight glitters off the honey to create a majestic play of dancing lights all around the room.

Princess Debbee and Prince Bob Bee look up in wonder. They're not allowed in the working area too often, as they're still pretty young to participate in what it takes to keep a beehive working properly.

They reach a small room, the little bees sit down, and the Queen begins the lesson.

"You see, all of these female workers leave each day to gather pollen and nectar from flowers to bring it back to the hive."

"That sounds like a lot of work," says Princess Debbee.

"They are definitely busy bees. Each day they might fly several miles from the hive just to get nectar."

Prince Bob Bee jumps up and down in excitement. "That sounds like a lot of fun! Why can't I do that when I get older?"

Queen Bee pats him on the shoulder. "Because you're a boy bee and you're built for a different job, but one that's just as important. You'll grow into a strong drone who helps make more bees to make our colony bigger!"

The Queen looks at the time. She's a very busy bee and she has a lot of things to attend to. She turns to a worker bee and asks politely, "I've got a meeting with Big Bee. Could you take over the princess's lessons for me just for a bit?"

"Of course!" replies the worker bee. "Come here, kids. Today we're going to learn!"

The worker bee continues the Queen's lesson to prepare the princess for her future work. "What do you know about worker bees?" she asks.

Trying to be funny, Prince Bob Bee shouts, "You work!"

"Anything else?" The worker bee shows her long tongue to the little bees. "You see, I use my tongue to suck up the nectar from the flowers, and then I store it in two stomachs and carry it back to the hive like groceries in a grocery bag!"

Princess Debbee looks down at her own stomach in surprise, not having known there were a whole *two* of them.

"Then, when I get back from collecting nectar, I give it to a younger female bee called a house bee. She chews on it for about thirty minutes and then puts it into one of these wax tubes. That's how the honeycomb is made, and it's how we store the food we collect for the colony."

Princess Debbee tries to take notes as quickly as she can write. She doesn't want to miss a thing. As soon as she finishes, she looks up, eagerly waiting to hear more, until she notices that the door has been flung wide open.

A group of worker bees storms in and interrupts the lesson. They are all panting and fanning themselves. They're so overheated that their stripes have nearly melted off their little bodies.

"What's wrong?" asks the worker bee who was giving the lesson.

"It's so . . . so . . ."

"Hot!" the second worker bee chimes in.

The three rush to help the worker bees from collapsing. Prince Bob Bee goes to get water for the women.

"Where's all the nectar? You came back with nothing?"

One of the worker bees, still barely able to speak from the heat exhaustion, says softly, "We didn't even make it to the Fresh Meadow."

"That's right," the second one adds through panting breaths. "We almost burst into flames because it's so hot. None of us could make it. We had to come back."

The door to the classroom is quickly flung open and in walks Big Bee, the head honcho in charge of Honey Bee Operations. He doesn't look very happy. He angrily asks the worker bees, "And what are the bees supposed to eat without any nectar for today?"

One of the bees lifts her wings up to dry them in the wind. They look as if they're melting. The Queen steps in, trying to calm the situation. "Big, take it easy. We've got enough nectar to last us for a few days until it cools down."

"Actually, we don't," responds Big. "I have a letter from headquarters stating that, due to the low amount of honey production this year, if we don't meet the quota in two days, we'll have to shut down this hive."

Big throws a large folder onto the table and

the papers fly out in the wind that's entering
through an open window. Honey drips onto the
edge of one of the folders as the Queen picks
it up. The huge red X's all over the papers say
more than enough.
The Queen knows just how bad this situation is
and pauses for a second.

The whole room falls silent. Princess Debbee
and Prince Bob Bee look up at the Queen with
worried faces. "You can't do that!" they
both shout.

"We can, and we will," exclaims Big Bee. "Two
days to prove you're a real honey bee hive or
else it's stingers out." He waddles out of the
room and slams the door behind him.

Queen Bee quickly rushes to reassure the
workers and her children that everything

will be okay, as any great Queen would. "Not to worry, dear bees. I will find a solution. Our hive will continue! For now, please rest. You'll need your strength. Tomorrow we will try again." She stands up, straightens her crown, and regains her strength and calmness.

Princess Debbee takes note of her mother's strength and decides then and there that one day she will grow up to be a Queen just as strong and great as she is. She stands up just as her mother did, straightens herself out, and walks out of the room, following intently in her mother's footsteps.

As night falls onto the honey bee hive, sleepy little Prince Bob Bee and Princess Debbee are getting ready for bed. With sweet pajamas on and all tucked in to bed, the two are read a story by King Buzz before saying their goodnights to their mother. Princess Debbee looks a little worried about the day's events, and the Queen asks what's bothering her.

"Are you sure everything is going to be okay?" the princess asks timidly but with such strength.

"Of course, sweetie," her mother replies, gently patting her antennae.

Princess Debbee, still not convinced, pushes the question further. "You're really not worried about what Big Bee said?"

The Queen smiles and relaxes into her grace. "As Queen of this colony, I don't have time to worry. It is my job to work on a solution, as we always do."

Once again, Princess Debbee admires her mother's strength and responds, "You're a good Queen. It must be so hard."

"Oh, honey. You will be a good Queen, too. You've got what it takes."

"Yeah, if she can just get over her fear of flying," Bob Bee mumbles under his breath.

"I'm not scared!" Princess Debbee almost jumps out of bed to swat at her brother. "I just need more practice . . ."

The Queen quiets the children, kisses them goodnight, and turns the light off. Prince Bob Bee turns over and over in his bed. He can't get comfortable. Faint music starts to play. It gets louder and louder. Both bees sit up. A bee bursts into the room with a boom box playing the Buzzy Bee Bump. He's got sunglasses on in the dead of the night and a large chain made of honeycombs around his neck. He turns the music up and dances past the two bees' beds.

Princess Debbee shakes her fist at the bee and shouts, "DJ Bee! We're trying to sleep. We have a big day tomorrow!"

DJ Bee plops down on Bob Bee's bed.

"Yeah, didn't you hear?" asks the little prince. "Big Bee wants to shut down the colony."

DJ Bee can't sit still. In between bopping his shoulders and feet, he remarks, "That stinks!"

Princess Debbee gets out of bed and turns the music off. "You don't seem to care," she says.

"This is really important."

DJ Bee is so relaxed, he certainly doesn't see the problem. He never does. The truth is that he's usually too lost in his music to ever notice what's going on around him.

"Well, if it's so important," DJ Bee starts before finally setting the boom box down, "then why don't you just fly to the Fresh Meadow tonight to bring back the extra nectar?"

Prince Bob Bee looks shocked at this suggestion. His eyes pop out of his head and he gasps, covering his mouth to mask the noise. He turns toward his sister.

Princess Debbee pauses for a second. "Now? At night? In . . . the dark?"

"Yeah," replies DJ Bee. "It's cooler now than

it is during the day. It's the perfect time to fly! Your mom and dad won't send workers out because nobody wants to work during the night, but if you go fast you can be back before they even wake up!"

"What a silly idea," says the princess, crossing her arms and getting up to pace around the room. "How am I supposed to bring nectar back if I don't even have the right tools?"

Prince Bob Bee jumps out of his bed in excitement and begins to pace in the opposite direction of his sister. "He may have a good idea! You heard the worker bee today. She has two stomachs. I'm sure you do, too."

DJ Bee comes up and smacks Princess Debbee in the stomach. She smacks him right back in his stomach and then all three of the little bees stop to stare at her stomach, as if pondering whether or not this could *really* work.

The princess breaks the silence and turns away from the two boys and says timidly, "Worker bees train for bee years just to be able to make it to the Fresh Meadow. What if I can't make it?"

"Okay. You're scared. That's fine. I'm sure your mom won't be disappointed in the future Queen," DJ Bee says playfully, teasing the worried little princess.

"I'm not scared!"

"Prove it," says DJ Bee, challenging the princess. "I dare you to fly to the Fresh Meadow tonight."

You see, Princess Debbee has always been scared of flying alone. However, she really wants to save her colony. Big Bee said they had two days to find more honey, and if she goes tonight, she can make it back before morning so the worker bees don't have to fly in the heat again.

What do you think she should do?

You're right! She should go to the Fresh Meadow and try to save the colony!

Because she's scared of the dark, like a lot of us are, she's going to take her handy bumble light with her so she can see in the night sky.

Princess Debbee packs her back for the journey and prepares to head out the door. She looks back at her little brother and sees a worried look on his face for the first time ever. She goes over to him and pats him on the head. "Don't worry, Bob Bee. I'm a princess. Taking care of the colony is what our family does!"

"I know," the little prince says quietly. "It's just . . . I heard of something at school once that could be very dangerous for you."

Princess Debbee rolls her eyes. "Not *those* stories."

"You've heard them, too? About the Honeycomb Destroyer?"

Princess Debbee turns around slowly. "No, I haven't heard *that* one. It sounds scary. Why did you have to tell me right before I leave to save the colony?!"

Prince Bob Bee feels a little bad, as he thought his sister knew about the Honeycomb Destroyer. Everybody in his class at his school has heard of it.

"The legend goes that there's a big huge hand, but not like a normal bee hand. It's got five finger things. And they say that sometimes in the Fresh Meadow it comes out of the sky and grabs honeycombs. Nobody knows what happens to them after that. The Honeycomb Destroyer takes them and they never see them again."

Princess Debbee shakes her head in defiance even though her antennae are shaking. "I'm not scared." She looks back at her stinger as it shakes. "I'm going to be Queen one day, and that means I can't be scared. I've got to save the hive!"

And with that, Princess Debbee's stinger begins shaking so hard that she flies high up into the sky. She waves down at Prince Bob Bee and DJ Bee before grabbing tight onto her backpack and heading straight into the night. Lightning bugs swirl past the little princess as she barrels through tall wildflowers. The stars shine bright in the night sky as she conquers her fear of flying alone. Princess Debbee smiles as she flies on to save her colony, nodding at the lightning bugs who are guiding her to the Fresh Meadow.

Soon, she begins to tire. She flies lower and lower until she plops down into a luscious, green opening. Tall flowers surround her and she leans against one of the stems to catch her breath. Crickets chirp as the moon shines down onto the little bee's tired face. She doesn't have much time to rest, but that's okay because she doesn't want to.

Princess Debbee stands up, looking around in awe at the beautiful flowers and plants. This is her first time out of the hive, and she never knew that things could look so beautiful and vibrant. She approaches the flowers and tries to smell them, but they're three times her height.

"Is this what flowers smell like?" she wonders out loud. "Oh my, how sweet! I guess . . . I guess I should try to get the nectar out."

Princess Debbee tries to climb the towering stem of the flower, but she soon hears rustling in the grass below her. A figure comes bolting out of the blades and knocks her off the stem. "Hey!" she shouts. "I'm trying to pollinate!"

A tall, strong figure emerges from the grass behind the flower. It's another bee. But Princess

Debbee has never seen him before. He doesn't look quite like the drone bees she knows from her own hive. He must be from another colony nearby. He dusts off his chest and approaches the princess.

"Sorry, kid," he says as he extends his hand to shake hers. "I don't have time to stay and chat but - wait, you're *what*?"

"POL-LIN-ATE," shouts Debbee.

The bee shakes his head and begins to laugh. "Not like that, you aren't. What kind of honey bee are you?"

Princess Debbee stands up and dusts herself off to do a curtsy. "I'm actually a princess. Princess Debbee, pleased to meet you."

The bee steps back, pretending to be

surprised. "Oh, me. I had no idea I was in the presence of royalty." He mimics the princess's curtsy and tries to do a silly hand wave. He's clearly not from the same colony. He may not be from any colony, in fact. He plops down beside Princess Debbee.
"For real. What are you doing out here in the meadow, kid?"

"So this *is* the Fresh Meadow!" exclaims the princess.

"Well, I wouldn't call it *fresh*, but it's definitely the meadow." The bee sniffs the air. Yellow steam wafts out from above the petals of the towering stems above. "Smell that?"

"Oh, yes! These flowers smell absolutely lovely!"
"No, that's not the flowers. It's the rain."

The yellow steam begins to intensify. The
humidity is increasing more and more with
each passing second. Or, at least, that's what
it seems like.

Sounds of a gentle rain patter in the distance.
A mysterious, brownish-white "rain" begins
to fall from the sky in the near distance.
Princess Debbee hasn't seen much rain in her
lifetime, but she knows this isn't what it's
supposed to smell like.
She looks at the other bee, and he quickly
grabs her and takes her to safety under a
tiger lily that closes around them to keep
them dry.
Princess Debbee peeks out from behind one of
the tiger lily's petals and asks, "This is rain?"

The bee shakes his head and pulls her back
under the petal, covering her mouth with a

small blade of grass to act as a mask.

"It's some type of rain, but it's not normal. I don't know what it is, but normal rain smells fresh and light. It waters the plants to help them grow. This rain seems to kill everything in the meadow."

"Even the bees?" asks the princess.

"Especially the bees."

Princess Debbee looks on in fright as the rain passes and the air begins to clear. She burrows her bee brow in worry as she thinks about her family and the other bees who fly to the Fresh Meadow so often to pollinate. Does her mother know how dangerous it is out here?
The bee coughs and distracts the princess

from her worries. You can tell he's had a cough for a while. Princess Debbee looks over at him with concern, as each cough sounds like it's coming from deeper and deeper inside of his tiny bee chest.

"Say," she begins to question, "how long have you been out here in the Fresh Meadow? Which colony are you from?"

The bee tries to shake the mysterious rain off the plants to prevent them from getting hurt. Despite being a little rough around the edges, he seems like a pretty nice bee.

He coughs a little bit more and then responds, "Oh, I don't know. A few bee years, probably. I left my colony a long time ago. Well, I wouldn't say *left* as much as, well . . . it's not important."

"Why would you do that, Mr. . . .?"

"McBee. McBee Light." He extends his hand to formally introduce himself to the princess.

"It's a pleasure to meet you, McBee."

"Anyway, I left my colony in search of a quicker way to make honey so that bees could survive longer without going out to pollinate every day. Then, one day . . . well, have you ever heard of the Honeycomb Destroyer?"

"It's real? And you've seen it here in the Fresh Meadow?" Princess Debbee asks, frightened.
"Oh, come on. You're not scared, are you?" McBee points to her stinger as it shakes ever so gently.
"No. I'm going to be Queen Bee one day, and that means I can't be scared. My mom, Queen

Bee, is *never* scared."

McBee laughs at this. "Of course moms
get scared, too! It's okay to be scared. The
important thing is that you don't let your fear
stop you from doing the things you want and
need to do."
McBee does a little twirl around Princess
Debbee, trying to scare her just for fun. "Well
then, she's never seen the Honeycomb Destroyer
up close!"

Princess Debbee takes a step back. "Is it *that*
scary?"
"Well, the first time I saw it, I had to dodge it
like this."

He jumps to the left on one foot.

"And then like this . . ."

He jumps to the right on the other foot.

"And then I had to run like this!"

McBee continues to demonstrate the little dance he did to escape the Honeycomb Destroyer. He leans down towards Princess Debbee and says, "Sometimes when I'm scared, I do these moves to remind myself that I'm strong and that I can face even the biggest of Honeycomb Destroyers! Can you do the dance with me?"

Princess Debbee nods her head confidently and stands up. She does the dance with McBee, smiling and laughing.

Soon, she realizes that all of her fear has gone. By replacing her fear with quick moves to escape the imaginary Honeycomb Destroyer, she's replaced her fear of the real thing!

However, she tires quickly and has to sit down.

"Whew. Running away from the Honeycomb Destroyer sounds exhausting. You've seen it more than once? What did it look like?" she asks McBee.

"Listen, kid. I don't really want to talk about it. Besides, you haven't told me what a princess is doing out in the Fresh Meadow alone."

The princess's face turns from glee to sadness as she remembers why she's there in the first place. "Our hive is in danger. We haven't been able to collect nectar because of the heat, which means no honey."

"So you flew here alone? My, that's impressive! I guess since you're royalty, and because you flew all the way here alone, you must be one tough little bee. I suppose . . ."

"What? You'll help me?"
"Well, I was going to say that I suppose you could join my team." McBee looks around him and takes in the silence of the meadow. "My team of one."

"Oh, but why won't you help me?"

"You haven't asked for my help. As a future Queen, you should know that it's important to ask others for help when you need it. There's no shame in needing help, but you should always be sure to ask nicely."

Princess Debbee pauses for a second, thinks, and asks, "Mr. Light, will you please help me and all of the other bees back at my hive? I'm out here trying to save them all, and I feel as if I might have taken on too much as only one little bee."

"Only if you promise not to be scared if we encounter the Honeycomb Destroyer."

Princess Debbee jumps up and down in excitement. McBee Light begins to walk off without saying anything and suddenly the princess realizes she's in the grassy opening all alone. She shouts out for McBee. He pops his head out from behind a blade of grass. "This way, kiddo!"

A bright yellow sun beats down onto the sweltering meadow grass. Smoke rises from the plants as the heat evaporates every little drop of dew that the morning left on the ground. Both McBee Light and Princess Debbee are panting from the heat. Their antennae are almost melting down the sides of their faces and they can barely walk any further.

Princess Debbee can't take it anymore. "How much longer?" she asks as she wipes the sweat from her face.

"It should be just through . . ." McBee pushes through some tall grass blades and opens the princess's view to a crystal clear blue lake. "
. . . here."
Princess Debbee rushes to drink the water. It's as if she hasn't had a drop of water in days.

"Not so fast, princess," McBee warns her. "You'll make yourself sick!"
She ignores McBee's warning and continues to lap up the delicious water. It's just what she needed and her tummy's getting full pretty fast. McBee takes a few drinks himself and

looks over at his little bee friend.

The princess falls back onto her hands as her stomach sticks out in fullness, her black and yellow stripes looking more stripy and balloon-like than usual.

"I told you not to drink too fast."

"What does it matter?" the princess replies. "It's not like we're going anywhere for a while. Let's just stay here and rest while I soak up all the hydration."

McBee Light shrugs his shoulders and plops down next to Princess Debbee. He turns to say something but instead gags. Princess Debbee looks away in disgust.

"*What* is wrong with you?!" exclaims the princess. Then she gags, too. "Oh, no. What an awful smell! Don't tell me it's that disgusting rain stuff again."

McBee Light covers his nose. He walks over
to a particularly dense patch of shrubbery
and peels away layers of grass until he finds
exactly what he thought he would: a honey
badger.

"Sorry, guys," giggles the honey badger
nervously. "I heard voices and I got a little
scared. Y-y-you know how scary it is out here
in the meadow all alone." He shrivels back a bit
into the grass to hide his face.
McBee shakes his head. "Honey Badger Harry.
Nice to see, uh, smell you again." He turns
towards the princess. "Princess Debbee, this
is Honey Badger Harry, the weirdest honey
badger I've ever met in my life." Honey Badger
Harry looks a little saddened by this comment,
but it's hard to tell if that's just his normal
face or not.
The princess looks at him curiously and

slowly approaches him to shake his big, clawed paw.

You see, honey badgers are known for being the most fearless creatures in the world. There's nothing, and that means nothing, that they are afraid of. That's what makes Honey Badger Harry such an odd little creature. He's scared of everything. And, the other thing you oughta know about honey badgers is that when they do get scared, they drop stink bombs.
"I can't make it one journey across this lake without smelling one of your awful stink bombs, Honey Badger Harry. When are you going to learn how to control your fear?" asks McBee Light as he waves the air around them to get rid of the smell.

The honey badger responds, "I'm working on it. Just this week I made it to the edge of the water

and was able to look at my own reflection
without startling myself! Paw step by paw
step, I'm making progress."

Princess Debbee is standing off to the side,
still speechless. She tugs on McBee Light's
arm and motions for him to lean down to
her. He does, and she whispers, "Don't honey
badgers kill bees?"
McBee Light stands up and directs her
attention towards Honey Badger Harry, who's
still shaking so much he's barely able to get
himself out of the little hole he'd dug himself
in the grass. McBee laughs.

"Yes, princess, normal honey badgers are very
dangerous to bees. Their scientific name, as
the humans call them, is *Mellivora capensis*,
which literally means 'bee-eater.' But, this
one? Honey Badger Harry? He's harmless.

He's like me. A lone outcast living out here in the Fresh Meadow in search of . . . well, I'm not quite sure what you're looking for, Honey Badger Harry."

As he's talking, McBee helps the honey badger get out of the thick of the tall meadow grass.

"Nothing really," responds Honey Badger Harry. "I've just always been this way. A little different. Storming honey bee hives and eating all of the eggs just always seemed like too much commotion to me. The noise, the aggression, the taste. Yuck. I'm shivering just thinking about it."

"You see," mentions McBee as he turns towards the princess, "we're all a little different, and that's okay. Honey Badger Harry's doing just fine out here. He's learned to co-exist with species he might not otherwise have had to get the chance to know. Like me."

"You're my best friend, McBee," says Honey Badger Harry in the sweetest little honey badger voice. As a bee, it's a little hard for Princess Debbee to take him seriously, as honey badgers are traditionally known for the ways in which they conquer and destroy beehives all over the world.

If it weren't for his soft, smooth voice, she probably would have run away by now.

"Okay, Honey Badger Harry. Let's not get ahead of ourselves," McBee responds nervously. What would Princess Debbee think of a lone bee out in the meadow with a honey badger as a best friend?

"Don't worry, Honey Badger Harry, I'll be your best friend if he won't," says Princess Debbee confidently as she walks over to sit next to the big beast.

McBee gives in, smiles, and sits down next to the other two.

What a sight. One big, scared honey badger and two tiny bees sitting on either side of him. Princess Debbee laughs at the adventure she's having. If only Prince Bob Bee could see her now. She's not scared of anything.
Just then, there's a loud CLAP! The ground shakes.
Princess Debbee's stinger shakes in fear and Honey Badger Harry grabs onto the two bees, almost as if protecting them.

This time, it's thunder. Real rain is on the way and it's noticeable as the sky begins to darken. Clouds swirl and form around them very quickly. The air begins to cool, and the little bees look refreshed.

Honey Badger Harry picks the two bees up ever so gently, each one on a different little claw. He carries them slowly towards his tiny burrow,

which is actually strikingly clean for a honey
badger home.

Little drops of rain begin to fall onto his back
as he sets Princess Debbee and McBee Light
down into safety.

"Thank you so much, Honey Badger Harry,"
says Princess Debbee courteously. Manners
were one of the first lessons she learned as
part of her training to become Queen.
Honey Badger Harry nods and scoots his way
into the burrow next to the bees. The rain
begins to pour, heavier now, as the thunder
beats down and shakes the entire Fresh
Meadow to the core.

The truth is that this rain is exactly what
the meadow and all of its inhabitants need.
It helps cool down the entire ecosystem

and gets rid of all of the bad air circulating
around the plants and animals.

Despite how refreshing it feels, it still scares
Princess Debbee and Honey Badger Harry
just a bit. McBee looks over at the two, who
are shivering as if they're cold. He knows it's
fear. He smiles gently at the both of them.
He's scared of things, too, you know, and
that's okay. Everybody gets to be scared of
something.
"They told me it was going to rain," says Honey
Badger Harry quietly, still shaking. What is
this honey badger *not* afraid of?

McBee looks over at the princess first, then
at Honey Badger Harry. "Who told you that?"
he asks.

"Oh, the bees. There was a whole family of them
flying around here earlier."

Princess Debbee shoots McBee Light a quick look
and jumps up, equally excited and worried. "Who
were they? What did they look like?" She asks
frantically, thinking for sure that a few bees
were left behind from the last group that flew
out here.

Honey Badger Harry pauses for a few seconds,
thinks slowly, and finally responds, "Well, there
were three of them. No, four. Wait . . . three."
"Just get on with it!" Shouts McBee Light.

Honey Badger Harry snarls his honey badger
teeth at McBee. He actually looks like a real
honey badger, which frightens Princess Debbee
and even McBee a little bit.

Honey Badger Harry stops himself and
immediately goes back to looking like his sweet
old self. "Sorry," he says, ashamed. "Sometimes

when I feel threatened, my true honey badger nature comes out."

Princess Debbee pats him on his side and tries to reassure him. "Sorry, Honey Badger Harry. I think what McBee meant to say is that I've got friends and family who live in a hive nearby and they were out here earlier."

McBee tries to help. "Yeah. It was so hot, though, they they never made it all the way to where they needed to go. They had to head back to their hive due to the heat."

Honey Badger Harry nods at this information. "Yes, yes. I know all about it. The Queen and King told me. Nice little family, except for that annoying little boy bee."

"Bob Bee?!" shouts the Princess.

"Yeah," replies Honey Badger Harry. "How'd you know his name?"

"That's my family!"

"You are royalty, too? Wow, what are the chances? I've met so many royal bees today." McBee Light looks stunned at the fact that Honey Badger Harry still isn't connecting the dots. He waits for a second to let the light turn on inside the honey badger's head.

"Wait a second . . . if you're royalty too, and the royal family was around here earlier . . . then why are you here and not with them?"

"There's no time to explain. Our hive's in trouble and I came here to help. Did they tell you what they were doing here?" presses the little princess.

"Well, they said they were looking for
. . . oh, you."

McBee Light screams out in frustration. "Geez,
Honey Badger Harry! Which way did they go?
Were they okay? Did they say anything else?"
Just then, a voice echoes from across the
lake. It sounds like . . . could it be another bee?
A booming echo shoots across the water, and
there's a sudden flutter of wings, buzzing, and
black and yellow stripes.

A little bee comes crashing down into Honey
Badger Harry's burrow, hitting him right in
the belly.

"Bob Bee?!" the princess shouts excitedly.
"What are you doing here?"

Prince Bob Bee comes buzzing out of the water

in the lake, doing a backflip as he goes. He is
followed by King Buzz and Queen Bee.
King Buzz wipes a water droplet off his wing
and replies, "No, sweetie. What are *you* doing
here?"

Princess Debbee rushes to hug her parents,
still not quite believing that they're actually
there with her.

"We have been worried sick about you," Queen
Bee says firmly as she hugs her daughter
close to her.

"How did you know where to find me?"

Prince Bob Bee butts in, "I couldn't keep it a
secret. The rain made it all the way to the hive
and everybody had to take cover. As soon as
it passed, I got too scared and told Mom where

you had gone."

"Then, we met this fellow here," says King Buzz as he motions towards Honey Badger Harry, who's hiding in the back. "Gave all of us quite a scare."

Honey Badger Harry lifts his little clawed paw up and waves at the royal family.

"It was all very noble of you, honey," says the Queen to her daughter, "but please don't ever do it again."

"Yes, sweetie," the King chimes in. "I flew the family here as soon as I heard. Why would you do such a silly thing?"

"I just wanted to save the hive. I thought if I did, maybe you would all think I was a good princess."

"We already do," reply both of her parents at the same time.

The king comforts his daughter. "But since we're all here now, we might as well solve the problem. As a family."
McBee has been standing off to the side watching the whole family reunion take place. He bites down onto a blade of grass and starts to walk off. "Well then, I guess I'll be off! Honey Badger Harry, until next time!"

Princess Debbee rushes to stop him before Queen Bee chimes in, "Oh, me. I'm so sorry. How rude of us! We're the Royal Buzz family, I'm the - "

"The Queen!" interrupts McBee. "Yes, the princess has told me about you. Nice to meet you all, but I really have to get going."

"You're not a honey bee from around here, are you?" questions the King.

"Well, technically, I am from around here, if by *here* you mean the Fresh Meadow. This is my home!" McBee spins around, does a little dance, and motions with his hand to show off his "home," the Fresh Meadow.

"This guy is funny. I like him," says Prince Bob Bee before mimicking the dance that McBee has just done. He stops suddenly and his antennae shoot up into the air. "Ew, I think I'm going to be sick. Does it smell a little like that rain to you guys?"

Before the family has the chance to react, McBee and Honey Badger Harry help huddle them all under some nearby flowers. They

make sure that none of them get wet,
protecting them just as McBee protected the
princess earlier.

The family makes it safely under the flowers
and the King asks, "What *is* this stuff? I've
never seen anything like it before."
"We don't know," replies McBee while coughing,
"but it hurts the plants."

"And the bees!" shouts Princess Debbee as the
rain pounds harder down onto the meadow and
the Buzz family.

Queen Bee, behaving in her typical queen
manner, tries to calm the family down. "Don't
worry," she says while bringing her children
closer to her. "It will be okay! Don't let the
rain touch you and we'll all be okay."

The rain passes and the meadow heat rises
once again. McBee hops out from under the
flowers to try to shake the rain off the
greenery before it hurts them. He coughs and
coughs and coughs.

King Buzz walks over and pats him on the
back. "Thanks for protecting my family. Is
everybody okay?"
"I'm fine!" shouts Bob Bee.

"I am, too!" says Princess Debbee.

"Yes, sweetie," replies the Queen as she heads
over to help McBee.

"It's getting dark," says the king as he looks
around. "We should rest for the night. Do you
have a place where we can sleep?"

"Sure, I'll take you to my camp," McBee
answers. "We've just got to follow the Golden
Honey Road." He looks over at Honey Badger
Harry and raises an eyebrow.

"No, no, no. No, Sir. You know that's far too long
of a journey for me."
The Buzz family laughs and hugs their strange
new honey badger friend before they head off.

"Let's follow the honey, everybody!" Queen Bee
grabs her children by the hands and prepares
herself for the journey.

The family takes off, hand in hand, with McBee
at their side. Even though they have had a lot
of trouble and scary moments, they skip and
hop their way down the delicious Golden Honey
Road, dipping their toes into a stream of
bright yellow honey as they go.
They know that sometimes a journey can be

difficult, but that doesn't mean they won't accomplish what they came here to do.

The group finally makes it to camp and starts a campfire. The orange firelight glows across their tired faces as they all sit down to eat their dinner from a can. McBee, the last one to sit as he was busy preparing their food, begins to tell a story.

"So, one day, a blanket flew from the sky onto me while I was sleeping. I was so cold, with it being winter and all, and I had been dreaming of a warm, cozy blanket all night. Next thing you know, I wake up and - BAM! There's a blanket!"

The family leans in closer as they become more interested in the story.

"I looked at the blanket on top of me and saw

that there was strange writing on it. I tried to hold it up against the moonlight so I could read it properly, but it was written in human and I couldn't understand much of it. I've slowly been learning, though."

"What did it say?" asks Bob Bee, eagerly following the story.

"It was talking about bees."

"Was it from the Honeycomb Destroyer? Was it a trap?" questions Princess Debbee skeptically.

"Maybe, or from a whole group of Honeycomb Destroyers. It seemed like a guide on how to take the hives from the meadow."

"And do *what* with them?" asks King Buzz.

"I couldn't tell from the writing, but I did see the Honeycomb Destroyer one day. It's not a monster or an animal. It's brown and big and dirty, and it reached into the Fresh Meadow and grabbed a honey bee hive."

Queen Bee gasps. "That's worse than Big Bee wanting to shut down our colony! I can't allow that to happen. Think about all of the bees depending on us!"

"Yeah," the Princess chimes in, "we have to do something."

"I think I might know of a way to fight the Honeycomb Destroyer and save your colony," says McBee as he huddles the family together. "Listen up."

McBee whispers his plan to the family as the moon begins to fade and the sun stretches its arms over the Fresh Meadow. A new day begins, and the Buzz family is prepared to fight for their colony.

In between yawning and stretching and a few groans from the prince and princess, the Buzz family and McBee begin to pack up their camp. They have gone over the plan one, two, three, many times and they're all prepared for what they have to do.

Princess Debbee looks over at McBee, who looks a little more tired than the rest. She walks up to him and places her tiny little bee hand inside of his.

"Thanks for helping us," she says. "It means a lot to us. To me."

He smiles at her, relaxing for the first time in a while, and says, "It's what I came out here to do. Well, to find a way to help my own colony. I was never able to do that, but now I can help you and your family."

"Well, we're going to do it together! We'll defeat the Honeycomb Destroyer, get the honey, and save our colony. I know it."

King Buzz interrupts the heartfelt session. "Is everybody ready?"

"Ready!" they all shout as they strap on their backpacks and gear.

Princess Debbee takes McBee's hand once again, and he gives her a little smile. "We're ready," he says, as each member of the family takes their position at the base of a flower.

"Remember what I said about pollinating?" he asks.

"That only female worker bees can do it," Bob

Bee replies.

King Buzz looks at his wife and daughter and asks proudly, "Ready, ladies?"

They both respond at the same time, "We're ready!"

Princess Debbee and Queen Bee climb up the flowers to begin pollinating. They suck the nectar out with their tongues just like Princess Debbee learned during her lessons. She's so happy to be beside her mother doing this, and she feels like a true princess for the first time.

McBee takes King Buzz and Princess Bob Bee to the side in a huddle. While the Queen and the princess continue to pollinate in order to bring back enough nectar to the colony, they will ensure they stay safe and hydrated. But

there's also another part to the grand plan.
You see, to defeat the Honeycomb Destroyer they
have to get his attention first. They have to stop
him from taking any more hives, which means
they've got to call him to the Fresh Meadow to
distract him before defeating him once and for
all.

Prince Bob Bee looks hesitant. "I don't know, guys.
we're calling the monster right to us."

"It's what we have to do," says King Buzz
reassuringly, "to ensure that the colony and all
the other beehives stay safe."
McBee pulls out the paper blanket that landed on
him many nights ago. He begins to try to read it
to the others.

"If you look here, it says that he's allergic to
bees. I think." He makes a face. He's not so good at

reading human words.

He points to a part of the paper showing a picture of a bee stinging a man with a large red X over it.

"While they are collecting nectar to take back to the colony, we've got to draw the Honeycomb Destroyer towards the Fresh Meadow. Once he's here, the Queen will take the nectar back to your colony, and the princess will sting the Honeycomb Destroyer in the neck."

"It's the perfect plan!" exclaims Prince Bob Bee.

"Everybody in their positions then," says McBee as he checks to make sure Princess Debbee and the Queen are doing okay.

McBee, King Buzz, and Prince Bob Bee fly up to

the top of the blades of grass to create a loud buzzing noise. They flap their wings furiously and the rising sun bounces light off of them to create a bright reflection across the Fresh Meadow. The harder they flap their wings, the louder the buzzing gets.

"Keep going!" shouts McBee over the loud buzz.

Prince Bob Bee stops for a second. "Did you see that? Over there!"

In the distance, a large figure appears. Its shadow covers the morning sun and the entire Fresh Meadow becomes darker. It takes one step and the meadow shakes. Another step, more shaking. Prince Bob Bee stares with his mouth wide open.

"Don't be scared, Bob Bee!" Princess Debbee

shouts from her flower. "Keep going! You can do it!"

"Louder, boys!" shouts McBee. "We've almost got him!"

Princess Debbee continues to gather nectar for her colony amidst the bright purple, yellow, and orange of the beautiful flowers that cover the Fresh Meadow. Queen Bee is right by her side, and she takes a moment to look over at her daughter and remind herself just how proud she is of her. Soon, they've collected enough nectar.

"Mom, take it back to the colony before it's too late. Don't worry, I'll take care of things here!" Princess Debbee insists.

Meanwhile, above the fresh blades of meadow grass, the scene looks a little bit different. The sky darkens as the Honeycomb Destroyer gets

closer and closer. McBee stands his ground. He
continues to flap his wings harder and gives
King Buzz a thumbs up.
King Buzz takes his son's hand and reassures
him that everything will be okay. Prince Bob
Bee looks down at his sister and gains more
strength.

The Honeycomb Destroyer is so close to the bees
now, and with Princess Debbee done collecting
nectar, she can go to help the rest of her family.
She flies up to where Prince Bob Bee is and
begins to flap her wings hard, too.
The Honeycomb Destroyer's hands come close to
the two little bees. McBee tries to distract him
by flying past his ear.

The Destroyer begins to wave his big, gloved
hands around the bees, swatting here and
there to try to stop them from buzzing so loud.

Another clap. King Buzz flies around to the back of the large figure's big suit and swats him in the back of the head.

Princess Debbee buzzes around the big hands coming to catch her. She can't quite reach the neck. She gears up to run towards the hands and sting them before one comes down and crushes her.

The others gasp, and there is a long pause followed by total silence. A voice booms down from the sky, "Now, what is a little bee like you doing all the way out here alone?"

The Honeycomb Destroyer leans down and looks at his hands. It is the face of an older man. McBee shouts, "She's not alone!"

"Oh my," says the older man, surprised. "You talk?

Something moves from under his hands. A small

voice shouts from underneath, "Yeah, and if you don't let me go right now, I'll sting you!"

He opens his hand gently to reveal an angry Princess Debbee. She stands up, straightens her clothes and her antennae, and crosses her arms.

The Honeycomb Destroyer, who is actually no destroyer at all, says gently, "I never meant to hurt you. I just wanted to stun you a bit so you wouldn't hurt me first! Besides, don't you know that you'll die if you sting me?" Princess Debbee looks up at him, actually curious about what he's just said. "Is that true?"

"Of course it is. All honey bees with stingers die after stinging humans. You only have one chance to sting, and I don't think you should use it on me."

"Don't listen to him," says McBee, stepping in
to protect the princess. "He's the enemy."
"Enemy? My, my. You must have the wrong guy!
I'm a beekeeper. It's my job to protect you all!"

McBee brings out the paper and points to
the picture of what they thought was the
Honeycomb Destroyer. "But isn't this you?
You're the Honeycomb Destroyer. You're
the one who takes the hives from the Fresh
Meadow and destroys them all."
"The what?"

"Excuse me," the king says as he intervenes,
"I'm King Buzz, pleased to meet you. Are you
not the monster who has been destroying the
hives in this meadow?"

"Destroying, no," the beekeeper chuckles and
his face brightens up. He no longer looks

Princess Debbee gets really close to the beekeeper and asks, "Then why do you try to hurt us?"

"Not all of us do. On behalf of all humans, I want to say sorry if any of us have hurt your hives. I am one of the good ones, though! Our Earth is a delicate place to live, and sometimes humans do things that affect us all."

"Is that why it's so hot out here?" asks King Buzz as he sits down in exhaustion from the "battle" that just took place.

"I'm afraid so," the beekeeper responds as he fans the king. "You see, we humans have hurt the atmosphere by not taking good enough care of it. It causes the temperature to get hotter and hotter over time due to a thing called global warming. Our actions have an effect on even the tiniest of animals, and

that's why I come to the meadow every so
often to check up on you guys. When I see a
honeycomb that's in danger, I take it back to
my sanctuary just to keep an eye on it."
Prince Bob Bee has a realization. "So that's why
nobody ever sees the hives again!"
"You were trying to help us all along,"
Princess Debbee chimes in.
"That's right," the old man says, shaking his
head, "and I'm sorry if I scared you."

King Buzz, still trying to piece the puzzle
together, asks about the mysterious rain.
"That's actually why I've been trying to move
your hives. The Fresh Meadow has been taken
over by farmers using something called
pesticides. While pesticides are good for
certain things to grow, they are harmful to
the environment and to bees like you."

King Buzz thinks for a second, and just as

he's about to say something, Queen Bee lands
gracefully amongst the others.

"If you took our hive back to your sanctuary,
could we make honey in peace? Would all of our
bees be safe?" The Queen has been listening
to the entire conversation and has made her
decision.
The beekeeper smiles and bows down to greet
the Queen. "Yes, you have my promise."

"Then, it would be my honor to introduce
you to our kingdom," says King Buzz as he
straightens his crown and reaches out to
shake the beekeeper's large hand. "Follow us!"

The group of bees, now accompanied by the
rather large, tall figure of the beekeeper,
follow the Golden Honey Road back to their
hive.

They travel through the towering green forests of grass and wildflowers, down the honey-coated hills of the honey bee lands, and through the jungles of sweet, dripping vines. And, finally, they arrive back home. Home sweet home. Has it never looked *so* sweet?

The beekeeper sets them all down and lets them enter the hive while he waits behind a tree, not wanting to startle the little bees inside the colony.

He can't help but peek out onto the tiny little hive. He's so excited. Saving hives is his life's work, after all, and the chance to save yet another colony would be a great moment for him as a beekeeper.

King Buzz and Queen Bee are welcomed back to the hive with open arms, as are Prince Bob

Bee and Princess Debbee. The entire hive has been waiting patiently for their return. They quiet all the bees and wait until they are attentive to explain what's just happened. Worker bees and drone bees alike look on in horror, excitement, and delight. The expressions on their faces vary from happy to sad, yet there is one emotion that they cannot hide. They all look towards the little princess as she stands timidly next to her mother and father.

As the story unfolds, the bees lean in closer and closer and look on in excited delight as they hear what Princess Debbee did to save the hive.

"And that's how we got back here. The gentleman is waiting outside," finishes Queen Bee.

Silence. Every single bee has its mouth wide open in awe. Then . . .
CHEERING! SHOUTING! SCREAMS OF EXCITEMENT!

The bees swarm the royal family and lift Princess Debbee into the air. She lets go of her mother's hand as the Queen smiles. She can't help but shed a tear, one single small droplet of pride at the young woman her daughter has transformed into.

She lets her daughter go as the colony carries her off and allows the princess to enjoy being the hero for the first time in her life.

As the excitement settles down, the hive begins to prepare for the move. The beekeeper will transport the entire hive to his sanctuary where all the bees will live in peace with the resources they need to survive.

As everybody prepares for the move, McBee begins to pack his back to leave. Princess Debbee tugs on King Buzz's shirt and points to McBee. Her father nods and she goes over to talk to him.

"McBee! What on Earth are you doing?"
"Well, I'm getting ready to head out. I've got to get back . . . home. Well, to the Fresh Meadow at least," he responds.

Princess Debbee shakes her head and laughs. "This is your home now!"

"This isn't my colony. I don't want to force myself into your hive."

"That's nonsense," says the Queen as she approaches them with snacks for the journey. "This is your hive, too. You're family now."

"Yes, it would be an honor to have you stay here. You saved my family and our home. You looked after our princess," King Buzz says while patting McBee on the shoulder.
"Well, actually, it was the princess's strength and determination mostly," says McBee. "She's one strong bee."
Princess Debbee smiles. "It takes a whole colony to make a honeycomb thrive, not just one bee!"

"Yes, sweetie," says the Queen. "That's why we all have to work together."

"Including with the humans!" shouts Bob Bee as he sits atop the beekeeper's shoulder.

"Yes," confirms King Buzz, "especially with the humans."

Princess Debbee steps forward. She's looking at you. Yes, *you*!
"Did you hear that? We're ready to work with you all! If you help protect the environment and keep us safe, we can all live in peace to make this Earth a better place for everybody." The entire Buzz family, McBee, and all of the bees in the hive join hands and prepare for their journey to the sanctuary with the beekeeper. They wave as they head off into the golden sunset, happy to have found harmony with humans once and for all.

CPSIA information can be obtained
at www.ICGtesting.com
Printed in the USA
LVHW071511300721
694156LV00022B/1521